PARIAH

A Play About Outcasts
Living Among Outcasts

by Lowery Christopher Collins

PARIAH

A Play About Outcasts
Living Among Outcasts

by Lowery Christopher Collins

Ponderlake
Publishing

PARIAH,
A PLAY ABOUT OUTCASTS LIVING AMONG OUTCASTS

Written by Lowery Christopher Collins

Ponderlake Publishing: www.ponderlake.com

Playwright and/or Royalty Information: www.ChristopherCollinsOnline.com

ISBN 978-0-9992241-8-2

Pariah
by Lowery Christopher Collins

Cast (in order of appearance):

Hannah Holloway—a young woman in her twenties, a loner, a reader, an independent spirit

Bo Holloway—Hannah's slightly younger brother, extremely dependent, fearful, emotionally down-trodden

Connie Holloway—Hannah's and Bo's mother, gruff, selfish, bitter

Ezekiel Warren—middle-aged, maybe older, owner of the local storage-building units, a doomsday prophet

Tom Ortiz—an observant, stand-offish businessman, the owner of the local marina

Oscar Shay—a middle-aged man who has seen emotional pain, a former boxer

Manny Shay—Oscar's son, late twenties, possibly thirty, victim of a weak heart ailment and of other problems, hard-working, decent, but troubled with strange visions

Willa—around thirty, owner of a local boutique

Odom—a recent release from prison, works at the Lake Shiloh Country Club Clubhouse

Julian Fletcher—late thirties, a wealthy, has-been, B-movie actor who has retired to Lake Shiloh

Regina—forties, Lake Shiloh's most prominent and busy citizen, involved in every town function, a drunk

Claus—fifties, a wealthy immigrant from Germany

Sally Mae—forties, a local woman with tattoos all over her face, Claus's girlfriend.

Joey Argo—twenties, recently (and too-soon) released from a hospital for the mentally disturbed, the son of the town's wealthiest man, who also happens to own the Lake Shiloh Country Club

PARIAH

Time: *Sometime during your lifetime*
Place: *Somewhere you have been—the town of Lake Shiloh*

Scene 1: *A small field next to a lake.*

Oscar walks downstage left and addresses the audience. Music swells, as it may at various points in the play.

Oscar. Did you ever see a man walk on the water? Did you ever see a man walk on the water? Not the Son of God, but an ordinary man, with flesh and blood and with his sins upon him? Did you ever? It's the question I ask.

(He walks offstage. The lights come up downstage center. A young woman, Hannah, is sitting there looking up in awe over the audience as if she is looking at the sky. Her mother and brother enter from stage right and stop.)

Bo. There she is, Momma. Over there. *(He points at Hannah.)*

Connie. Just what I thought. Sitting there, staring at the stars like some nutcase. Wasting what little time we have. Staring at God knows what.

Bo. She's just looking, Momma.

Connie. Dreaming, like a fool.

Bo. Momma . . .

Connie. Go and get her. Get her back to the house. I've wasted enough time out here. I got things to do.

Bo. She's just sitting there and . . .

Connie. Go and get her. Don't argue with me. *(She leaves.)*

(Bo runs up to his sister, Hannah.)

Bo. Hannah!

Hannah. *(She screams a little scream.)* Bo. Don't do that. You scared the life out of me.

Bo. You gotta come on. Momma's blown a gasket and getting madder by the minute.

Hannah. Where is she?

Bo. Over there. *(Points.)* Walking home. Her blood's boiling.

Hannah. She was here?

Bo. Yeah. She sent me over to fetch you home. She's not happy. Said her time was wasted again.

Hannah. Bo, look at these stars. It's been a long time since we've had such a clear night. And the stars are almost bouncing off the water.

Bo. Hannah, did you hear me? We've got to go home.

Hannah. I mean, all there. Each group so clear and vivid. Some bright, some dim, some twinkling to beat the band.

Bo. Are you listening to me? I'm going home.

Hannah. Calm down. Look, will you? It's the stars. They've been out there forever. Take a second and look.

Bo. *(Looks.)* Yeah, they're there. They twinkle. They're downright beautiful. We gotta get home now, though. Come on, Hannah.

Hannah. Momma calls. The world stops spinning when Momma calls.

Bo. I'm leaving now.

Hannah. I'm coming. *(She stands up.)* Are the stars out tonight? I do believe they are.

Bo. *(Takes Hannah by the arm.)* We are, too. But we're going home. Come on! *(He leads her offstage. She looks back at the stars before exiting.)*

Scene 2: *A sidewalk in front of a drug store.*

Two men, Ezekiel Warren and Tom Ortiz meet casually.

Ezekiel. *(In a strange, happy way)* Tom Ortiz! I haven't seen you in months. How are you? *(Holds out his hand.)*

Tom. *(Friendly, but not as excited)* I'm good, Ezekiel. How are you?

Ezekiel. Can't complain. Not a bit. Things are as they are, won't be for long, but can't complain.

Tom. I see. *(Chuckles.)*

Ezekiel. I tell you. Things are going well, soon they'll go to hell, but for now they're going well.

Tom. *(Obviously put off a bit, but hiding it well)* Business going well? People renting storage buildings?

Ezekiel. Like nobody's business. It's a sign of the times, I say! People have so many possessions, so much junk they don't need that they don't have room for it all. Their houses are so full of material things that they don't have room for everything, so they come to me, Ezekiel Warren, purveyor of space, landlord of tiny units where they can store all those things they can't bear to part with, but they have no room in their daily lives for. It's amazing. I am there to help though, to supply a need, to take their money month by month. It's a sign of the times, I say.

Tom. Well, people do have so many things that . . .

Ezekiel. That's the problem. So many things. So many things. Someday those things will all burn. It's not far away. Don't ask me what will happen, but something will, and all their houses and lands and possessions will melt like wax in an oven. But until then, I provide a service.

Tom. *(Put off)* Okay. Makes sense to me, Ezekiel. If I need a storage unit, I'll make sure to keep you in mind.

Ezekiel. The best there is, as long as time—as we know it—continues.

Tom. Good. Well, have good afternoon.

Ezekiel. I intend to. I want to enjoy whatever we have left. *(He walks off without a good-bye.)*

Tom stares at him as he walks away, then walks off in a daze himself.

Scene 3: *On the Holloway front porch.*

Hannah sits, reading a book. Connie, her mother, exiting the house, joins here on the porch.

Connie. There you sit again. Wasn't it enough that you had to drag me and your brother all over Creation last night to get you home in time to help? Now you're sitting out here as pretty as you please, reading a book?

Hannah. I'm just reading, Momma. I got most everything done in there.

Connie. Most everything ain't everything, now is it? Wasting time like a no-good bum, filling you head full of crazy notions—like your father. I worked my best to make sure your brother didn't act like him, and now my own daughter is . . .

Hannah. Momma, please, I'm just . . .

Connie. Don't interrupt me. I am your mother, and you'll listen to every word I say or to every moment of silence I choose to give you.

Hannah. *(Getting irritated.)* Momma . . .

Connie. *(Angry)* Don't interrupt me, I say! Or you'll find yourself on the streets.

Bo enters from the house.

Bo. I got the furniture moved and the wood stacked by the back of the chimney.

Connie. I am talking to your sister here.

Bo. I was just letting you know that I got it all done.

Connie. Go do it again.

Bo. What?

Connie. Move the furniture back.

Bo. I just moved it all where you told me to.

Connie. Don't sass me. I won't have one lazy good-for-nothing in my house, much less two. Get in there and do what I said. And you, Hannah Holloway, get rid of that book before I toss it in the fireplace. Get in there and clean the kitchen.

Hannah slowly stands, puts the book under her arm and begins to walk off the porch, into the yard. Bo stands dumbstruck.

Connie. *(Angrily)* Hannah!

Hannah stops, closes her eyes, turns around and slowly enters the house. Connie points to the door and addresses Bo.

Connie. Go!

He follows his sister.

Connie walks to the front of the porch, closes her eyes for a minute, begins to cry a little, violently wipes the tears from her face, pulls out a cigarette, lights it, and begins to smoke. The lights fade on her.

Scene 4: *A local café.*

Oscar Shay sits at the counter, drinking a cup of coffee. A young man, his son, Manny, in his twenties, sits at a table, also drinking coffee, voraciously reading a newspaper. Willa, a benevolent young woman, around thirty, enters, notices them and approaches Oscar.

Willa. Mr. Shay, how are you, sir?

Oscar. Willa, I am doing great. How are you, young lady?

Willa. Oh, you charmer. "Young" and "lady" in the same question.

Oscar. *(Laughs)* I call 'em as I see 'em.

Willa. Very few people have your vision, sir.

Oscar. Oh the blind who will not see. *(They both laugh.)*

Willa. So, things have been going well?

Oscar. They have been going. Is that enough slide from being great?

Willa. Fair enough. How's Manny? *(She looks over at Jake.)*

Oscar. I don't know. He's okay I suppose. He had a hard day at work, and when he came home, he was real hungry, so I offered to buy him a burger and a cup of coffee. He ate in record time and started reading again.

Willa. Still having visions?

Oscar. Don't say that too loud.

Willa. Sorry. I was just wondering.

Oscar. I know. I know. I'm sorry. People just don't take to that too well.

Willa. I understand.

Oscar. But to answer your question, yes. He doesn't tell me a lot, but yes, he's still having 'em.

Manny. *(Getting up with the newspaper)* Dad. Look what I found in the paper. *(Notices Willa)* Oh, hi, Willa. I didn't see you there. How are you?

Willa. I'm fine, Manny. You okay?

Manny. Yeah. I'm okay. *(Thinks)* Yeah. I am a-okay.

Willa. Good.

Manny. Dad, look what I found in the paper: one of those lawnmowers with the side blades. Right in the ads. Somebody's wanting to sell theirs. Cheap.

Oscar. *(Looks at the paper)* Really? I'll have to look into that.

Manny. Mr. Griffin has a guy mow the area in front of the lumberyard with one of those, and it does a fine job, a fine and dandy job.

Oscar. Well, I'll have to look into that then. I will.

Willa. You feeling okay, Manny?

Manny. Pardon?

Willa. I was wondering if you're feeling all right.

Manny. I am good, Willa. I told you.

Oscar. Willa's just concerned. Just . . . curious.

Manny. Oh.

Willa. I'm sorry. I meant no harm.

Manny. I'm okay. No harm done. *(Looking ahead into nothingness as if having a vision)* No harm done. No harm done.

Oscar. Manny? What's happening? We need to get out of here. You . . .

Willa. Is he . . . ?

Oscar. Come on, Manny.

Manny. As the day wanes and the night approaches, the tree will glow in the shadows.

Oscar. Come on, Manny.

Willa. Manny, Mr. Shay.

Oscar. Help me get him to the door.

Willa and Oscar get on either side of Manny.

Manny. The glow will permeate the shadows and illuminate the darkest areas.

Ezekiel enters the café.

Ezekiel. What's going on here?

Willa. Excuse us, Ezekiel. We need to get by.

Ezekiel. What's happening here?

Oscar. Please let us by.

Ezekiel. Oh, the Visionary Boy is having a revelation I see. Seeing into the future again, Manny Shay? Images of things to come haunting you again?

Oscar. Ezekiel Warren, let us by and leave us be. I need to get my boy home.

Manny. The shadows quake as they are revealed.

Willa. Manny!

Manny. *(Takes Ezekiel by the arms and stares at him)* And those tremble who dare not be exposed.

Ezekiel. Get your hand off of me, freak! Liar and freak.

Oscar. Hold your tongue.

Oscar and Willa take Manny offstage.

Ezekiel. There's not room for two visions, boy! The end is near! Hell will fall on the earth! And when it falls, I'll be here. I will call it down if I need to. And the first piece will destroy all liars! And false visionaries!

Scene 5: *The same field from earlier.*

Hannah leads the way. Bo follows.

Hannah. We're almost there.

Bo. Hannah, we need to go home. I don't want to listen to Momma gripe and yell.

Hannah. Bo, whatever you do, Momma gripes and yells.

Bo. Hannah . . . *(Stops)* Well, yeah, that's true.

Hannah. Of course it's true. Look! Here it is. From here, you can see nearly into forever. Look over there, Bo, beyond the dam.

Bo. *(Still nervous)* It is quite a ways. I'll bet that's the next county.

Hannah. Or the next.

Bo. Heck, we might be looking right over the state line.

They both laugh.

Manny enters from stage left, unaware of Bo and Hannah.

Hannah. *(Hearing his walking)* What's that noise?

Bo. Who's there?

Manny. Does it make a difference that I'm here?

Bo. What does that mean? Who's there?

Hannah. Does it make a difference? What?

Manny. That I'm here.

Bo. It might. Who is it? Is that Manny Shay?

Hannah. Manny Shay?

Manny. Yeah, it's Manny Shay.

Bo. What are you doing out here?

Hannah. Bo. People have a right to roam freely.

Bo. Not to sneak up on people.

Manny. I'm not sneaking up on anybody.

He walks closer.

Hannah. What are you doing walking around out here, Manny Shay?

Manny. I could ask the same question of you.

Bo. Stay away from us, you freak.

Hannah. Bo!

Bo. I mean it, Shay. I've heard that you've been having your visions and nonsense. Just stay away from us. We don't need to be around your kind.

Hannah. Bo, what's gotten into you?

Bo. You haven't heard about Manny Shay, with his visions and prophecies? Going into his trance, seeing things, scaring people to death?

Hannah. No.

Bo. Well, it's true. He's going around pretending to be something he's not, scaring the whole community. You keep it away from me and mine.

Manny. I don't intend to bring anything to you and yours.

Bo. Just stay clear.

Manny. I'm just walking. Not messing with anybody.

Hannah. Bo, leave him alone.

Bo. Don't defend him, Hannah. He's an outcast.

Hannah. Bo!

Manny. It's alright. I'm an outcast.

Bo. Yes, you are.

Manny. And what difference does it make that I'm here?

Bo. Enough.

Connie. (*from offstage*) Bo! Hannah! Where are you?

Bo. Hannah, we need to go.

Hannah. We were here to see the view.

Bo. We saw it.

Hannah. Not enough of it. We don't have enough time to see it all.

Bo. Come on, Hannah. We have to go. (*Starts to leaves and reaches for her.*)

Hannah. I'm not ready to go.

Connie. (*from offstage*) Bo! Hannah!

Bo. We have to go.

Hannah. No.

Bo. (*Leaving*) Hannah.

Hannah. No.

Bo. (*Walking away, addressing Manny*) You stay away from my sister.

Bo exits.

Manny. Aren't you going to go?

Hannah. Not yet.

Manny. You'll get in trouble.

Hannah. Trouble finds me. I've learned to not let it bother me. It's going to come whether I like it or not. Why fret over it?

Manny. You're quite the philosopher, aren't you, Miss Holloway?

Hannah. Philosopher? (*She laughs.*) Hardly. I'm just a girl who's learned the way things work. I happen to know what's real, and I happen to appreciate beauty. (*She looks intently at Manny.*)

Manny. (*Shivers slightly*) So, how've you been?

Hannah. That's quite a question.

Manny. What?

Hannah. How've I been?

Manny. Yeah.

Hannah. You've been back at Lake Shiloh for how long now? Weeks? And this is the first I've seen of you?

Manny. I've been working.

Hannah. Is that the only answer anybody gives anymore? Working, working, working! You'd think this world is nothing but work, work, work. There's more to life, Manny. (*Pauses.*) If I didn't know any better, I'd think you were trying to avoid me.

Manny. Avoid you?

Hannah. I do believe you are.

Manny. (*Walks slowly toward her*.) I have no reason to avoid you.

Hannah. You don't? Leave me for three years. No way to know if you are alive or dead. I call that mistreatment.

Manny. I had no choice. That's the way Dad and I live. I take care of him, like he's always taken care of me. We went with the work. You must admit, Lake Shiloh doesn't have a booming economy.

Hannah. Don't criticize Lake Shiloh. It's just about one of the most beautiful spots in the . . .

Manny. (*Interrupting her*.) I'm not criticizing. It's a great place, but it's a resort town. And I don't want to be waiting tables when I'm fifty. Besides, we've always been nomads. This is the only place I've lived twice. And with the new lumberyard and all . . .

Hannah. Okay, okay. Let me look at you. (*She holds him gently by the upper arms*.) Are you all right?

Manny. What do you mean?

Hannah. Are you all right? Something doesn't seem right.

Manny. (*He pulls away a little*.) Everything's fine.

Hannah. Okay. (*Changing the subject*.) Answer me this: did you come looking for me tonight?

Manny. (*Laughing*) Time hasn't made you less conceited!

Hannah. (*Slaps him on the arm*.) Hey! (*Laughs*.) Answer me.

Manny. I was hoping you'd be here. I at least wanted to say hello.

Hannah. Hello?

Manny. Yeah, hello.

Hannah. Just hello?

Manny. For now, yeah.

Hannah. I don't know what to say. I mean, three years.

Manny. I was really expecting that you'd be married with twins or something.

Hannah. Me? Married? Not to anyone at Lake Shiloh. I love this place, but the men don't exactly knock down my door asking me out.

Manny. They're crazy.

Hannah. That you've got right! And they think I am. That's the problem I guess, but I tell you: I'm glad they don't knock down my door. I'd have to knock them down a peg or two. You?

Manny. What?

Hannah. You? You're not . . . involved?

Manny. Nah. I, uh, well, no. There's nobody.

Hannah. But there was?

Manny. It was nothing. A silly fling. I can do silly things at times.

Hannah. But this wasn't silly, was it?

Manny. (*Suddenly*) No! Not at all.

Hannah. Because I know that . . .

Manny. No, no. This was not silly.

Hannah. Good. Because I was, well, I mean, we're actually not far from . . .

Manny. I know. Don't worry.

Hannah. Don't worry. (*Smiles.*) That's pretty much impossible. I put on a good front. Everyone gets quite irritated with my, let's say my, upbeat view of life, but, in here (*She puts her hand on her chest*), I juggle the world. (*Pauses.*) What visions was Bo talking about?

Manny. Forget about it, Hannah.

Hannah. I want to know. What was he talking about?

Bo. (*From afar*) Hannah, come home!

25

Manny. Nothing.

Bo. Hannah, get yourself here now. Momma says to get home.

Hannah. Something *is* different, Manny. Something's going on.

Bo. (*Entering.*) Hannah, Momma . . . (*notices Manny*) You're here. I told you to stay away from my sister.

Hannah. Bo, shut up.

Bo. Momma wants you home.

Hannah. Momma always wants me home.

Bo. Don't argue with her. (*Then to Manny*) I'm warning you, Shay. Don't come around her.

Manny. I don't take too well to warnings.

Hannah. Bo, this is nothing to you.

Bo. It's everything to me. Stay away from her. We've heard way too much about what you are.

Manny. You don't have the slightest clue. (*Steps toward Bo.*)

Bo. (*Steps back.*) Stay away, freak.

Hannah. Bo!

Connie. (*from offstage*) Bo! You found Hannah?

Bo. Hannah, go home. Please.

Hannah. I don't want . . .

Bo. Please. Momma wants you.

Connie. Hannah! Are you out there?

Hannah. (*Angry*) Yes!

Connie. Get home now! Bo! Hannah! Now!

Bo. See?

Hannah. Manny, ...

Bo. Please.

Hannah. Manny, I'll see you . . .

Bo. No.

Hannah. Butt out, Bo. Manny. Later. (*She holds out her hand and runs home.*)

Manny. Later.

Bo. No. No more laters. (*He runs home.*)

Manny. Later.

Scene 6: *Lake Shiloh Country Club*

Odom is rubbing down the counter. Julian Fletcher enters.

Odom. Mr. Fletcher, how are you today, sir?

Julian. I am fine, Odom. Just thought I'd take in a few rounds of golf before the storms get here.

Odom. Storms? Are we in for some bad weather?

Julian. Yes. It's all over the news. It'll be here in the next few days, but I still want to some play in before the grounds are soaked for a week.

Odom. I hadn't heard.

Julian. Like I said, it's all over the news. But again, you're probably not used to television, having lived without for all those years.

Odom. We had TV., Mr. Fletcher. It was just in the meeting rooms. We didn't have them in . . . .

Julian. . . . the cells?

Odom. Right. (*Quiet*)

Julian. (*Pauses.*) But enough about unpleasant pasts. I am thirsty enough to drink all of Lake Shiloh.

Odom. The usual?

Julian. No. I am trying to cut back. How about a tonic and water?

Odom. Tonic and water then.

Julian. Yes, I have self-control. I am a professional. I can choose how much alcohol I drink.

Regina enters.

Regina. Did someone mention alcohol?

Julian. Welcome to Lake Shiloh Country Club.

Odom. Your tonic and water. (*Places it in front of Julian*)

Regina. Julian! Tonic and water! Are you crazy?

Julian. No. Are you drunk?

Regina. Never, love. Never.

Julian. Never.

Regina. Tonic and water? What a waste of good tonic! It partners with gin, Julian. With gin!

Julian. I'll remember that.

Odom. Without it, it's just GIN-ny in a bottle! (*Begins laughing*)

They both stare at him.

Regina. Let me order you a real drink, Julian, our own private little movie star.

Julian. No, thank you. I'm cutting back, trying to do without it a while.

Regina. You are out of your mind, Mr. Brando?

Julian. Please, Regina. I'm no Brando.

Regina. One Manhattan, Odom. And don't put anything that resembles water anywhere near it.

Odom. Yes, ma'am.

Regina. No Brando, pshaw! Brando wishes he had starred in *Rage of the Lion Man, Rage of the Lion Man 2, No Room for Guns, Ninjas in Paradise Valley* . . .

Julian. Regina, please . . .

Regina. *Rage of the Lion Man 3, Art is Just a Name, Saving the Whales is for Sissies.*

Julian. Regina, please. I've left all that behind for an early retirement, to play some golf, enjoy the lake.

Odom. Your Manhattan, Ms. Regina.

Claus and Sally Mae enter. Claus is European, and his lover Sally Mae is a proud "redneck" with tattoos on her face.

Claus. (*with a German accent*) Ah, Mr. Julian Fletcher. Ms. Regina Jackson, we thought the clubhouse would be empty this time of day.

Regina. Claus, how are you? (*She hugs him daintily*) And Sally Mae, my little tattooed . . . friend.

Claus. Regina.

Sally Mae. Ms. Regina, how is running the town going?

Regina. It's a tough job, but . . . well, you know the rest. (*She takes a drink of her beverage.)*

Julian. (*Stepping forward to shake hands.*) Claus. Sally Mae.

Claus. Julian. Planning a little golf before we get so flooded that we can't play for weeks?

Julian. (*To Odom*) Great minds.

Sally Mae. How are you, you rich movie star?

Julian. I wish you all would forget that I made movies. I'm just a resident of Lake Shiloh, a nice, calm . . .

Sally Mae. Forget? Never in a million years, not after that scene where we got to see your whole butt in *Rage of the Lion Man 3*. I'll never forget your . . . talent.

Regina. That's right. We can't forget that we have a rich celebrity right here in Lake Shiloh!

Claus. You Americans are something else. Fame and fortune. Lifestyles of the rich and famous. *(He sits, as if at a café table.)*

Sally Mae. In Lake Shiloh? (*Laughs*.)

Regina. Yes! Lake Shiloh is home to impressive people. We are an outstanding community. And that's part of the reason I want to ask you something, Julian.

Julian. Will I need the gin with the tonic? (*He sits.*)

Odom. Gin, Mr. Fletcher?

Regina. It's not that bad. Julian, the counsel and I want you to speak at the Lake Shiloh Founders' Day Festival next Friday. Just a few words. You know—since you're our most famous resident.

Claus. Ah, Julian. Speaking at town festivals! Not a, what you say, Oscar speech, but the next best thing.

Julian. I'll have to think about it. It's sudden notice.

Regina. Just a few lines. You're happy to live in Lake Shiloh. This community has so much to offer everyone. We have some of the best people in the state living along the banks of our little man-made lake.

Julian. Why don't you give the speech?

Sally Mae. That sounded so good.

Regina. I can't give the speech. It wouldn't look right.

Odom. Don't you speak every year?

Regina. And how would you know? You've been away for three or was it four?

Claus. Ya. She has spoken every year since I moved to this lovely community.

Regina. Well, as chair of both the city counsel and the lake-area chamber of commerce, the president of the historical society, and the wife of the president of the country club, I do have a sort of first citizen's obligation to vocally trip the light fantastic at certain events. (*She drinks.*)

Sally Mae. She has such a way with words.

Claus. *Ja.*

Regina. C'mon, Julian. Six, seven sentences. Think of it as an acting role. After the Lion Man, it should be a breeze. Surely you had small, but important, roles in high-school one-act plays or something. Be nostalgic. Just be Julian. Just be you.

Joey enters. It is obvious he is mentally disturbed. He even "leads: with his over-opened left eye with everything he does.

Joey. Just be me. Just be me.

Claus. God help us.

Odom. (*less than excited*) Joey.

Regina. (*kissing up*) Joey, how are you, love? Feeling any better?

Julian. Rather bold, aren't you, Regina?

Claus. You're just now noticing that?

Regina. (*Ignoring them*) And how is your father?

Joey. Froggie went a-courtin', and he did ride, um-hm, um-hm.

Sally Mae. Not much change.

Regina. Of course there is. That's a good song, Joey. Is your father around? I need to talk to him about the festival.

Joey. Festival! Yeah. Dad's here. He's, uh, uh, talking to the valet.

Regina. All right. That means he'll be in shortly.

Joey. (*looking up to the ceiling, yells in frustration and confusion*) NO!

Regina. What? What's wrong?

Joey. Oh, nothing. I'm just thinking.

Claus. God help us.

Joey. Uh, well . . .

Claus. (*to Odom*) Rum and coke, Odom.

Sally Mae. (*to Odom*) Make that two.

Regina. (*to Odom)* Three.

Joey. I'm sorry. Before they let me out, Dr. Barring told me how to control, my, uh, my outburst of, uh, well, um, frustration, I guess. That one just slipped by. I'm sorry, uh, I guess.

Julian. (*to Odom*) Make it four.

Joey. (*to Sally Mae*) Oh!!! Um, um, Sloppy Jean, um, Susie Lynn, um, um, . . .

Sally Mae. Sally Mae. Sally Mae.

Joey. Sally Mae. Sally may do what? (*He laughs uncontrollably. Odom joins the laughter. They others stare at Odom. Joey pauses.)* What great tats on your face there, Lady Mae. The markings of the cruel world on the tender skin of womanhood.

Sally Mae. Well, thank you, I guess.

Claus. Let's change the subject, shall we? Is your father coming in soon, young man?

Joey. Subject change. Yeah. I just got out of the hospital. Um, but you're still a Kraut, a Jerry, right?

Regina. Joey!

Julian and Odom laugh uncontrollably.

Claus. Young man! I don't care if your father does have more money that the rest of Lake Shiloh combined. I will not allow you . . ..

Joey. But you are, right? Loyal to the homeland and all that?

Claus. My political leanings are none of your affair!

Joey. So, I'll take that as a "yes"?

Claus. You will take it as I meant it and I delivered it.

Sally Mae. We need to go, Claus. We really, really need to go.

Claus. I will not be manipulated and chastised by a . . .

Julian. Rich boy?

Regina. Claus, please. Try and stay calm. I need to talk with Mr. Argo. I don't need a fuss. This is a country club, not a common bar.

Joey. I saw Manny Shay today.

Regina. Pardon?

Joey. Manny Shay and his father were at the Burger Delight today. He had another vision.

Regina. Oh, did he?

Julian. A regular clairvoyant, isn't he?

Sally Mae. That boy scares me.

Julian. He's no boy.

Scene 7: *Willa's Gift Shoppe*

Regina enters.

Willa. Oh, Ms. Regina, hello. Welcome, welcome.

Regina. Thank you, Willa. How are you, dear?

Willa. Doing well. I haven't seen you in here in a while. Is there something I can help you with?

Regina. Just busy all the time, all the time. Doing this and that. Just needing a few tokens a few gifts for some of our speakers and organizers of the Lake Shiloh Founders' Day Festival next Friday. There is no better place in this town than Willa's little gift shop.

Willa. Thank you. Anything in mind?

Regina. Just looking, sweetheart. Just perusing the selection. (*Looking*) How quaint! How, unusual.

Willa. If you need anything, let me know.

Regina. I shall.

Connie enters.

Willa. Connie Holloway?

Regina. Connie?

Connie. Is there a problem? Am I not welcome?

Willa. No, it's not that! I just haven't seen you in a while. Not in here at all.

Connie. Well, I don't get around much. Stay away from the town and from the water. (*to Regina*) Miss Chamber of Commerce, you still staring?

Regina. Sorry, no. I'm just shopping. Haven't seen you in a while.

Connie. I'm here. Not exactly the same as when we ran around in high school, but here I stand.

Regina. Here we stand. (*laughs nervously*)

Connie. Yeah. (*turns away, looking*)

Willa. May I help you?

Connie. I came in here for an angel.

Willa. An angel?

Connie. Yeah, you had a little pink and white angel in your window about three months ago, and I wanna buy it.

Willa. Oh, well let me see if I can remember which one we had there. (*Looking*.)

Connie. Yesterday was my birthday, and my kids gave me money to get what I want, and that's what I want.

Regina. Oh, yesterday was your birthday? Happy Birthday.

Connie. Yeah, it was. Yours is October 4th. (*to Willa*) D'you find it?

Willa. I think I might have.

Julian enters.

Julian. Regina.

Regina. Julian, what are you doing here?

Julian. I thought I saw your Rolls out front.

Regina. It's not a Rolls. It's a Mercedes.

Julian. Whatever. I have two. It doesn't matter.

Regina. You shouldn't be here. I am buying small gifts for the speakers at the Lake Shiloh Founders' Day Festival next Friday.

Connie. You're Julian Fletcher, that movie star who can't act.

Willa. Oh my.

Connie. The one who moved here because he couldn't get more contracts without some sort of Lion Man in them?

Julian. No, my friend. I have merely retired from the craft.

Connie. Oh, was that it?

Julian. Aren't you the mother of that strange girl who reads her life away, sits by the lake, and is happy all the dang time?

Regina. Julian, perhaps we could discuss this, well, whatever you came to discuss out of doors?

Julian. I just wanted to tell you that Joey's right. I saw that Manny Shay guy and that boxer father of his at a gas station.

Regina. (*Nervous*) Julian, (*looking at Connie*) not here. Not now.

Julian. He was putting gas in their truck, and then he got this look on his face—like he was going into a trance. He said the coming rain is going wash away more than dirt.

Regina. Julian.

Julian. That boy's a freak. He and his old man. A regular pariah.

Willa. Mr. Fletcher, please.

Connie. (*Storming out.*) Keep your angel.

Scene 8: *Outside the Shiloh Marina.*

Ezekiel is walking with a fishing pool and a tackle box. Claus and Sally Mae exit from the Marina, but Tom shaking their hands.

Tom. I hope you enjoy the boat. It's about the best I have.

Sally Mae. We will, Mr. Ortiz. We will. I am looking forward to it.

Claus. We intend to enjoy ourselves tomorrow.

Ezekiel. What if there is no tomorrow?

Claus. I will have rented a boat for nothing then! (*He and Sally Mae laugh.*)

Ezekiel. This is no laughing matter.

Tom. Ezekiel, please. These are my customers.

Ezekiel. In Lake Shiloh, people aren't customers. They are people, just people. Stocking up on possessions galore. Things, money, society.

Claus. Ya, that's about right. Things, money, society. It makes the world work.

Ezekiel. Oh, such blind people.

Tom. I have to go back inside the marina. I have other customers. Thanks for your business, Claus, Ms. Sally Mae. (*He reenters the marina.*)

Ezekiel. Vile, marked.

Sally Mae. You talking about me?

Ezekiel. I am talking about everyone. We have lost our way. (*He continues walking.*)

Oscar meets him walking from the other way. Claus and Sally Mae watch.

Ezekiel. If it isn't the great fighting man! Oscar, the champ, or was he?

Oscar. Good day, Ezekiel. (*Continues walking.*)

Ezekiel. The boxing man who ended up in a circus somewhere, or am I hallucinating?

Oscar. (*Continuing.*) You research well.

Ezekiel. And the freak son of yours!

Oscar stops.

Ezekiel. Oh, I struck a nerve. (*Pauses.*) The freak son, having false visions. Scaring folks, scarring folks.

Oscar. You leave him alone, Ezekiel Warren. He hasn't done anything to you.

Ezekiel. He's a liar! A deceiver!

Oscar. Ezekiel.

Ezekiel. (*Mockingly.*) "As the day wanes and the night approaches, the tree will glow in the shadows. The glow will permeate the shadows and illuminate the darkest areas."

Oscar. Ah, you remember.

Ezekiel. Hogwash, malarkey, rubbish, genuine fabrications!

Oscar. Why are you so worried about it then? (*He walks off.*)

Ezekiel. You're a freak, too! Raising a freak like that! What man in is right mind makes a career out of beating people up! Then joins a circus! Freak!

Claus. Ezekiel.

Ezekiel. Father of a freak!

Claus. Ezekiel.

Ezekiel. What?

Claus. That man was a boxer?

Sally Mae. And was in the circus?

Claus. I thought they were new in town.

Ezekiel. New in town?

Sally Mae. They've lived here once before?

Ezekiel. Once?

Claus. Let me buy you, how do you say, a cup of joe, my friend.

Ezekiel. (*Going with them.*) Yeah, a boxer. A boxer.

Sally Mae. Are you coming to the Founders' Day Festival?

Ezekiel. And then the circus!

They exit inside the marina.

We see a flashback as a younger-acting Oscar scuttles to an imaginary boxing-ring corner. A manager, played by the same actor who plays Tom Ortiz, meets him there with a water bottle and a towel.

Manager. Oscar. Calm down, pal. Calm down. You don't wanna kill him! He's only human. He can take only so much.

Oscar. I know what I'm doing.

Manager. Just think it out. It's not a massacre. It's a sport.

Oscar. I KNOW WHAT I'M DOING!

Manager. You got a lot of pent up frustrations, pal. Just have fun with it. Don't be so brutal.

Oscar. This is what I do.

Manager. You need to focus in on his weaknesses.

Oscar. I know a man's weaknesses.

The bell rings. Oscar "dances" to the "ring." The manager leaves. Oscar, returning to his former age, slows, sits, and cries.

Scene 9: *Waterfront. It's during the day.*

Hannah enters, carrying a book. She finds a place and sits to read. As she is reading, we hear the voice of Sally Mae off-stage and then see her walking and looking, presumably for Claus. Hannah never tries to get her attention. Nor does Sally Mae ever notice her.

Sally Mae. (*Off-stage*) Claus? Claus? Are you out here? C'mon. I know how you are scared of all sorts of critters. (*She enters.*) Claus? Where on earth are you? You couldn't be that lost. We are getting into strange territory. The Holloway area, Connie and those two weird kids of hers? C'mon, Claus? Where are you? Just because that old doomsayer said that Manny guy roams these woods? (*She starts to leave.*) Claus? Claus? (*She leaves.*) Where are you?

Hannah stares out over the water (above the audience) and just smiles. She begins to read. Then she hears something.

Hannah. (*Whispering loudly*) Manny? (*Pauses.*) Is that you? Manny?

Joey appears, even crazier.

Joey. It's ain't Manny. I ain't no crazy fortuneteller.

Hannah. Joey. Just stay over there. (*She moves away from him.*)

Joey. What are you talking about, Hannah. I've know you since we were kids. Hell, I remember when you were as straight as a stick. Ain't that way no more.

Hannah. Okay, Joey. Just stay over there, please.

Joey. Aw. Don't be afraid of Joey. I was named after a baby kangaroo. Did you know that? I found that out in the hospital. That's why I hop along in life. I, um, well, I'm just walking along. I saw the Bavarian fellow and his whatever you call it, um, walking out toward past the public park and into the woods a bit, and I, um, well, I just wanted to see what they were up to. I didn't think about Hannah Holloway being out here. Hannah: always reading, always so happy. People wonder why you smile all the time, Hannah Holloway. It just ain't natural to be so happy. But, um, yeah, uh, then again, you ain't smiling now. You ain't happy to see me. I'm happy to see you. (*Pauses.*) Why were you calling that Manny guy's name? What's up with that? (*He moves closer.*)

Hannah screams. He steps closer. She screams louder.

Manny. (*from off-stage*) Hannah!

Hannah. Manny! Manny! I'm here! Help me.

Joey. Help you? (*Loudly and with his head help upward.*) Ugh! (*He runs off stage in the opposite direction of Manny's voice.*)

Manny runs onstage.

Hannah. Manny! (*She grabs him.*)

Manny. What's wrong?

Hannah. It was Joey Argo. He was here. And he was really scaring me, getting closer and closer.

Manny. (*Comforting her.*) It's okay. It's okay. Joey Argo? What was he doing here? He's out of the institution?

Hannah. Just don't let go. Please.

Manny. Okay. Okay. You never get scared.

Hannah. (*Calming down*) I know. I'm sorry. I just, well, I just had no control over what could happen. I always try to exert control, no matter what "things" happen to me. I try to remember that "this too shall pass" and things will get better, but that just, well, that just scared me.

Manny. It's okay. I'll have a talk with him.

Hannah. No, please don't. Let's just forget it. The last thing I want is an intentional visit from him. I think he just stumbled upon me, following some people that . . . . (*confused*)

Manny. What's wrong?

Hannah. I'm just trying to figure out what's happening here. People in the woods looking for . . .

Manny. Just calm down. It'll be okay.

She looks at him tenderly.

Hannah. You know where we are, don't you?

Manny. (*Looks around.*) By the lake?

Hannah. No. Think. Right here. This the place that you and I met that night three years ago.

Manny. Oh. Here?

Hannah. Yes, right here to be exact.

Manny. Oh, okay. (*Not nervous. Just detached.*)

Hannah. Don't worry. I never told anyone. Not even Bo. And he seems to follow me everywhere I go. It's a miracle he's not here now.

Manny. It's okay. Really.

Hannah. That was a special memory. It was so sweet and intense.

Manny. Nice words. Sweet. Intense.

Hannah. You know you are sweet and intense, Manny Shay.

Manny. Well, I wouldn't say "sweet."

Hannah. Aw, I would. Sweet as honey. (*Being romantic*)

Manny. Well. I, don't know what to say about that.

Hannah. You don't have to say anything. And don't worry. You know you were a true gentleman. You could have, well, you could have done a lot of things, but you didn't. You treated me with dignity, true dignity.

Manny. Well.

Hannah. But all that aside, we did have an evening to remember right on this spot. You know, like I said, I have nothing for the men of this town, Manny. Nothing. But you are so different.

Manny. So different. I know, Hannah. Are you, um, feeling better?

Hannah. I'm much better. I feel rather good again.

Manny. Good.

Hannah. You know we could have had a much more intense memory of this spot if you had not decided . . . to leave that night, if you'd not left. I mean, there is no one, Manny. No one. I never even knew if I'd ever see you again, or if you wanted to see me, and then you disappeared with your father into thin air. It wasn't that you weren't a grown man.

Manny. Things are complicated. My father needs me. I have to look after him.

Hannah. You're a grown man. (*Pauses.*) But there you are being sweet again. You had to do what you had to do.

Manny. Yeah. Not everything is simple.

Hannah. How I know that. (*Walking away, thinking*) It's never simple. You know, sometimes, I just wanna disappear from this world, wake up in one my books or in some exotic place. But then I realize that any place I'd go is filled with people longing to escape *their* exotic place. (*She laughs.*) People escape to Lake Shiloh. And here I stand, book in hand.

Manny. You understand it, Hannah. Life is the same wherever. But it's different, too. People are people. Problems, decisions, pasts to outrun: whatever. Just life.

Hannah. Just life.

Manny. I gotta get on to the house. Dad's expecting me. We're gonna mow a yard before sunset, get a little extra money.

Hannah. Thanks for being my knight.

Manny. I'm not a knight.

Hannah. (*She kisses him on the cheek.*) Today you were.

He walks off.

She calls after him.

Hannah. Go to the Founders' Day Festival with me next Friday.

Manny. I gotta go mow.

Hannah. At least think about it. It wouldn't any fun without you.

He exits.

Scene 10. *Outside the Marina.*

Oscar and Manny have been mowing. They are walking toward the front of the marina, but Manny doesn't feel tired enough to take a break.

Oscar. C'mon, Manny. Let's rest a bit.

Manny. I'm really not tired, Dad. We haven't been mowing that long.

Oscar. I know, but it never hurts to take short breaks, rest, get your wind.

Manny. All right. The marina's yard isn't that big. We can be finished in no time.

Oscar. I know. Sit. I wish we didn't have to do this all, but we need the extra cash.

Manny. Don't worry about it. People have to work.

Willa enters the scene from the marina. She is holding two glasses of water.

Willa. Gentlemen.

Oscar. Willa. I didn't know you were in there.

Willa. Yeah. I end up everywhere some time or another. Joe asked me to bring you two some water.

Oscar. Well, thank you and thank him.

She hands them the water.

Manny. Thanks. (*He seems to notice strange glances from her.*)

Oscar. (*Drinking.*) Cold, fresh water. Can't beat it.

Willa. (*Looking at the sky*) I thought we'd be drenched in cold rainwater by now. That front with all those storms just keeps brewing. It was supposed to be here yesterday. It keeps stalling and growing out west.

Manny. We don't watch much news.

Oscar. Sad to say. I didn't know one was coming.

Willa. Oh, yeah. One's coming. Inevitable I think.

Oscar. Seems that happens a lot. (*Getting up.*) I gotta get some oil from the truck. I'll be right back.

Manny. Need some help?

Oscar. Nah. I'll be back in a minute. (*He leaves.*)

Willa. You got a good father there.

Manny. Yeah. He's a good guy. Not perfect, but then again, I'm not either.

Willa. Well, he has a good son, too.

Manny. I don't know about that.

Willa. (*moving closer*) I have an idea.

Manny. You do?

Willa. Yeah. I've been watching you, Manny Shay.

Manny. Watching me?

Willa. Watching you.

Manny. And what have you seen?

Willa. Some things I like.

Manny. Oh, really?

Willa. Some things I like a lot.

Manny. Well, I do appreciate your attention and your complements, but I . . .

She reaches in and kisses him. Oscar walks back up.

Oscar. I seem to have returned a little too soon.

Willa. Uh, Mr. Shay. Um, I, I need to get back in to get the glasses back to Joe, and, um, go on back to the gift shop.

She leaves. But as she leaves, Oscar speaks.

Oscar. No need to be embarrassed, Willa. It's the way of life. It's the way of life.

Manny. She's gone.

Oscar. I see that.

Manny. Before you . . . (*He starts to have another vision.*)

Oscar. Son?

Manny. Water! When the water stops, when the water stops. And people stand all around, waiting.

Oscar. (*Nervous.*) Manny. Let's go home.

Manny. When the water stops, it will be over.

Oscar. Manny, come with me, son. We have to get home. You need to lie down.

Manny. (*Coming out of it, but weak*) What? What do you mean? We have the rest of the yard to mow.

Oscar. (*Putting his arm around Manny's shoulder and walking him home.*) Not today. The grass can wait.

Willa. (*Leaving the marina. She is holding her purse as if she is leaving.*) Manny? Mr. Shay. Is he all right?

Oscar. Yeah, we're just going home. It's been a long morning.

Willa. Did he just . . . ?

Oscar. We're going home, Willa. He'll be okay. (*She is speechless as they exit.*)

As soon as they exit, Claus and Sally Mae enter. It is obvious that they are incredulous about some information.

Sally Mae. Willa!

Claus. Willa!

Sally Mae. Willa, is that old Ezekiel out here? Somebody down at his storage place told us he was going fishing.

Willa. I haven't seen him. What's wrong?

Claus. What's wrong? It's that freak with the visions!

Willa. Freak?

Sally Mae. That Manny Shaw. He told old man Ezekiel something about a tree glowing at the end of day and that it would light up shadows or something.

Willa. Yes, yes, I was there. It was at the café.

Claus. You heard it?

Willa. Yes, how do you know he said?

Claus. The old man told us.

Sally Mae. Never you mind that! It came true!

Willa. What?

Sally Mae. It came true!

Willa. How?

Sally Mae. Last night, the Danforth house caught fire on the southside of Shiloh.

Willa. Oh, no.

Sally Mae. And it burned so hot that it caught their big old oak on fire, too.

Willa. The tree ablaze.

Sally Mae. That's not all.

Claus. The thought they had lost their twin little girls, but when the tree was at its brightest, they found them frightened, hiding in the shadows, shaking with fear and shock.

Willa is weakened.

Sally Mae. It came true. We just have to find the old man.

Claus. This is more than coincidence. We are going to talk with Regina as well.

Willa. How many people know of this vision or whatever you call it?

Sally Mae. Several people. Well, people the old man talked with and the people at the country club: Regina, Odom, and Julian.

Willa. Julian Fletcher?

Claus. Yes, but we can't tell him about the fire yet. He is out trying to find that strange, happy girl who reads all the time.

Willa. What?

Sally Mae. Oh, you know. That Holloway girl. Hannah.

Claus. I do believe he's trying to woo her.

Willa. Julian Fletcher wooing Hannah Holloway??

Sally Mae. Oh, she doesn't know it yet. He saw her at some store or something with her family. She doesn't get out much, you know. He was just smitten. Wanted to invite her to be his guest at the Founders' Day Festival. He said she is his new muse.

Willa. Hannah Holloway?

Claus. Ya, it is unbelievable, is it not, but stranger items have happened.

Willa. I, I have to get to the gift shop. We open at 10, you know.

Sally Mae. Yes, you go. Beware of that boy.

Claus. And beware of the storms. They are finally moving this way. They will be here by the morning.

Willa. I will. The storms. I will. (*She leaves.*)

Scene 11. *The banks of Lake Shiloh. Sunset.*

Manny is sitting, staring at the sky. Hannah approaches.

Hannah. Manny?

Manny. (*Startled*) Hannah. You surprised me. I didn't expect you at this part of the lake.

Hannah. It is true what they are saying about you?

Manny. What who is saying about me?

Hannah. Everyone. That your visions are coming true. That strange things are happening because of you.

Manny. Talk is talk. Don't believe what you hear. I learned that a long time ago.

Hannah. What am I to make of it all?

Manny. Make? Don't make anything. Know what you know. That's all we have.

Hannah. I'm so confused.

Manny. Look. The more you try to make of things, the more they make no sense. If I did that with everything that's happened to me, I'd be insane. I've seen and felt so much, that if I dwelt on it, I couldn't think at all. I don't understand a lot of things, and more than that, I don't understand me.

Hannah. Is that why you're here?

Manny. I dunno. I guess. Trying to think, well, not to think.

Hannah. Manny? Tell me about your mother. You have never mentioned her.

Manny. I don't talk much about things, Hannah.

Hannah. You live with your father and take care of him. Do you know anything about your mother?

Manny. I know she's not here. I know I barely remember her. I know that there're certain questions I was never allowed to ask. I know that she accidentally hurt me.

Hannah. Accidentally hurt you?

Manny. (*Smiling*.) When I was boy, she accidentally dropped some kind of pot or frying pan or something on me. She didn't realize I was under her feet crawling.

Hannah. What happened?

Manny. Oh, she realized it right as she tripped over me. A part of the pan hit me on the chest before she could knock it away. Left a scar. She didn't mean it.

Hannah. A scar on your chest?

Manny. Yep, in the shape of a giant drop of water. Strangest thing.

Hannah. May I see?

Manny. The scar?

Hannah. Yeah. Please?

Manny. I guess. (*He opens up his shirt to reveal a large teardrop-shaped scar on his upper chest.*) Nothing to it.

Hannah. (*looking*) Wow. It is like a drop of water.   Like a teardrop even.

Manny. Yeah. That's about the only story I know. It's not been something we've talked about. Even makes me a little uneasy doing it now. Let's talk about other things. (*Closing his shirt.*)

Hannah. I didn't know my father, either. And Momma won't talk with me about it, either. Well, Momma doesn't talk with me about anything really. I don't understand. There's so much more I deal with, too. So, I do understand.

Manny. So do I. (*Pauses.*) The water's calm tonight.

Hannah. Yeah, but a storm's rising. Everybody's talking about that, too.

Manny. Everybody talks about the weather, but no one does anything about it.

Hannah. Hey, I've heard that before.

Manny. Yeah, it's old. Very old.

Hannah. Manny, (*pauses*) I want you to know that someone tried to . . . seduce me today.

Manny. Seduce?

Hannah. Not in a violent way or anything like that, but he just tried to talk sweet to me, to convince me to go to the Founders' Day Festival Friday.

Manny. Who?

Hannah. You'll never believe this, but Julian Fletcher.

Manny. Julian Fletcher? That movie-star fellow?

Hannah. None other. He told me that he saw me in town, that I was beautiful.

Manny. Well you are very beautiful. (*Then realizes his words.*)

Hannah. Manny, that is very kind of you to say.

Manny. Well, thank you. I, I meant it.

Hannah. Well, you don't have to worry. I told him a flat-out no, that you and I were going to the festival together, that I wasn't interested in the slightest.

Manny. You told him that?

Hannah. I most certainly did. And don't fret, I know you haven't even told me if you are going, and that's okay. If you want to go, we will. If you don't, I don't want to go anyway. So, it's settled.

Manny. And Julian?

Hannah. He wasn't happy. I don't think he's ever been told no before. But I don't care. Movie stars don't mean a thing to me. So, it's over. The time for talk is done.

Manny. Hannah, today at the marina . . .

Hannah, Let's just sit, Manny. No talking. Everything's okay. You're right. Thinking can make things difficult. Let's just look at the beautiful, still water, just as the sun's setting.

He silently joins her, staring at the water.

Scene 12: *This scene takes place in three different places simultaneously: the Holloway front porch/yard, inside the clubhouse of the Lake Shiloh Country Club, and Willa's living room. Connie is on her front porch. Odom is working behind the counter of the clubhouse while Julian is at a table drinking, Willa in seated in her living room, reading. The wind is picking up; the storm is approaching.*

Odom. Are you all right, Mr. Fletcher?

Julian. (*clearly "tipsy"*) Did you say something?

Odom. I asked if you were all right. You're not saying anything. It's very unlike you.

Julian. Um, I'm okay. I'm just sitting here.

Odom. Yeah, but I wanted to make sure everything's okay. You're usually a person who has something to say about a lot of things, about . . . himself, and . . . um . . .

Julian. I'm not in the mood to talk, Odom. I'm just, I'm just here.

Odom. OH-kay. Okay.

Julian. I've, I've . . . (*pauses and then growls*).

Odom. Sir?

Julian. I've done a lot of things, Odom. I've lived life to the fullest. I've made a LOT of money. I've (*breathes heavily*) traveled the world over. I've had fame and fortune and women just throwing themselves at me and on me, but I've never had anybody reject me.

Odom. (*shocked*) Oh, oh, okay.

Julian. Don't act so surprised. I guess it happens to everybody. I just never thought of myself as everybody.

Odom. Well, . . . um, ...is it . . . somebody here at Lake Shiloh?

Julian. (*Pauses.*) Yeah. (*Chuckles.*) You could say that.

Odom. Well, um, I don't know what to say. I'm sorry. I don't know what else to say. I don't know any other comfort I can give other that saying: love stinks!

Connie: Hannah! Are you in that house? Or are you somewhere out in the middle of nowhere again?

Hannah. (*From inside the house*) I'm in here, Momma.

Connie. Well, get out here. I need to talk to you a little bit. And I don't wanna hear no sass or see you carrying no book. Just get out here and listen to me.

Hannah comes out on the porch.

Hannah. Oh, the wind sure is picking up!

Connie. Yeah, the storm's gonna be here pretty soon. They say it's blowing like crazy over in Brockton.

Hannah. It took a long time getting here. I guess storms eventually do arrive.

Connie. Yeah, they do, whether we want them or not. Sit down. I need to talk to you.

Regina enters the country club.

Regina. Oh! That wind is rough! Julian! Julian! Good, you're here. I've been looking for you everywhere. What's wrong?

Julian. Oh, nothing.

Regina. Oh, you're . . . drinking again! Good! Let me join you. (*Faster*) Odom, Odom, a . . . screwdriver!

Odom. Do you just go down the list alphabetically?

Regina. Just get a screwdriver, Odom. I'm not in the mood to argue with you. Julian, have you decided whether or not you're going to deliver a speech at the Founders' Day Festival?

Julian. Uh, I don't want to think about any speech.

Regina. I need to know if you're gonna do it. In fact, I need to know that your answer is yes.

Julian. You're one pushy woman. You just keep on twisting and turning like a . . . . .

Odom. (*Holding up her screwdriver*) Screwdriver!

Regina. (*Grabbing the drink*) Oh, gimme that drink. I'm not twisting or turning anybody, Julian! (Exhales audibly) Listen. I'm proud you're living in our community, and I want to show you off. And I've got something special to tell you, and I know this is supposed to be a secret, but I'm not one to keep secrets very often, so here it is. I don't mean this as an insult, but I am well aware that you aren't "Oscar" material. I don't mean it that way. (*Thinks*.) You're not the kind of person who makes all these artsy-fartsy films where people (*smirks*) learn "lessons" and all that. You're more of an action-adventure, kung fu, all that kind of stuff guy, the kind of movies that make money. Even though they're . . . not any good, they still make money. But anyway, WE have recognized the fact that you are a tremendous asset to our community, and we're going to give you the very first Founders' Day Honorary Citizenship Award, AND we have—are you ready for this?—none other than the president of the screen actors' guild from Hollywood, the man himself, stopping by here. He's gonna be sort of in the neighborhood, up in the city for some big meeting, but anyway, he's willing to make a slight detour to come down here to be the presenter of this award up on stage with ME—but only if you're gonna be there to accept it and to give your speech.

Julian. Robert's coming to Lake Shiloh?

Regina. Yes! He has promised to make a detour here. He hasn't seen you in a little while, and he just wants to . . . SEE you. What's wrong with you? I've never seen you down. You're never like this.

Odom. He's having personal problems.

Julian. Odom, I'll thank you to keep your mouth shut.

Regina. You tell the convict your personal affairs?

Claus, Sally Mae, and Ezekiel enter the country club; they are wind-blown and wet.

Regina. Oh, it's raining now? Oo! Oo!

Claus. Yah, it's raining. Don't worry about that. Have you heard? Have you heard?

Regina. (*Ignoring Claus*) Ezekiel Warren? What are you doing here?

Ezekiel. Ah, I see I'm not wanted in the materialistic element! I guess I need to go outside in the rain where I belong.

Sally Mae. Don't be silly. We brought him here. He is our guest tonight.

Julian. Ezekiel Warren's your guest. I didn't know you were friends.

Claus. It's a recent development.

Sally Mae. Listen, listen, listen. We have news. We have news.

Claus. Yah. We have information you might find interesting.

Ezekiel. Fraud! Charlatan! Downright spirit of evil!

Claus. Another one of Manny Shay's visions have come to pass.

Regina. No!

Sally Mae. Yes, ma'am. One he had at the convenience store near Bartleby and Myrtle. The one about the weeping lady who had lost hope—opening a door and, with a newspaper, blood would return???

Regina. (*Anticipating*) Yes?

Claus. Listen, listen.

Sally Mae. It was Gail Conroe. You know, she and her daughter, Amber, had a big fuss-to-do years ago, and Amber left. Remember?

Regina. Vaguely.

Sally Mae. That woman cried her eyes out. Every time, you'd see her, crying over Amber.

Regina. Okay, I know who you're talking about. Go on.

Sally Mae. She's just now starting to stop crying, realizing there was nothing she could do. She opened her door this morning to get her newspaper, and you'll never guess who was standing there, handing it to her!

Odom. Can I guess? (*Everyone ignores him.*)

Regina. (In disbelief) No.

Sally Mae. Yes, sir.

Claus. Yes, sir.

Sally Mae. Amber herself! "With newspaper, blood would return!" Her blood returned!

Ezekiel. It's not right! It's not! That boy is a menace!

Joey comes out of the shadows. Everyone is startled. Sally Mae screams.

Regina. Where'd you come from?

Joey. I've been over here. Just over here.

Julian. How long have you been there?

Joey. A few hours. Enough to hear a lot. (*Chuckles.*) I have ears. Some just have mouths. I have the ears. So the blood returned?

Ezekiel. No one is courageous enough to do what's right!

Willa is sitting as a knock is at her door. She gets up and answers. Oscar is there, in a poor-man's overcoat of some kind.

Willa. Mr. Shay! (*Highly embarrassed*) What are you doing here?

Oscar. I just wanted to stop by and have a few words with you, if you don't mind? If it's inappropriate, I understand.

Willa. No, no, no. Come on in.

Oscar. I didn't want to put you in any sort of compromising position. I just want to chat with you a few minutes. I would chat outside a little bit, where everything can be seen, but . . .

Willa. Oh, don't be silly! It's blowing like a typhoon outside, and it's going to start raining cats and dogs any minute.

Oscar. Yeah, I know. This storm's finally here. It's been forecasted for quite a while. Some people thought it wasn't going to show up, but it always does.

Willa. Yes, it always does, almost always. Have a seat, Mr. Shay. Have a seat.

Oscar. (*Sitting.*) I just wanted to stop by and talk with you a few minutes.

Willa. Ah, um, let me just be very blunt and say that I am very embarrassed.

Oscar. For what?

Willa. For what you walked up on at the marina this morning. That wasn't something meant for public viewing.

Oscar. That's not exactly my reasoning for stopping by, but it does have something to do with it. You see, Manny's at home asleep. He's not feeling too well. He hasn't talked a lot this afternoon because he's, well, having those frustrating visions again.

Willa. Oh, Mr. Shay. Don't . . .

Oscar. No, seriously, he's just stressed out and tired. I have no idea. I'm confused by it all. It's a confusing world we live in. Nothing makes a lot of sense to me.

Willa. I understand.

Oscar. But I do want you to know something. (*Pauses.*) If you and my son have intentions with each other, and if it's something that's been going on, something that you see happening, I just want to know your take on it.

Willa. Well, I don't know. I don't know exactly what to say. I don't know what Manny thinks.

Oscar. I don't either. That's why I'm here: to figure things out. He ain't talking, don't much anyway. He's sleeping right now.

Willa. He doesn't know you've come to see me?

Oscar. Not at all. I don't want him to know. I just wanted to hear it from you. I wanted to know exactly what's going on. You seem like a very nice young lady, and I wanted to see what's happening.

Willa. I don't know exactly what's happening, Mr. Shay. All I know is that I like your son.

Oscar. Well, it was premature of me to come here. It was out of place on my part. I just wanted to get out of the house a minute. You see, Manny hasn't had many girlfriends. He's spent most of his time following me around and taking care of me. It's not something that I'm proud of, but I guess I've robbed him of a life.

Willa. I'm sure that's not true, Mr. Shay.

Oscar. Oh, yes it is true. I'll be the first to admit it. I've not been the best father in the world. I've been a little demanding at times.

Willa. Mr. Shay. You don't have to . . . .

Oscar. Let me talk. I don't get to say this very often, and it's something that—if you are serious about my son—you need to hear.

Willa. Okay.

Connie. I've heard you've been hanging around Manny Shay.

Hannah. What?

Connie. You heard me. I heard you and that Shay boy have been enjoying nature together.

Bo walks up and hides at the edge of the house.

Hannah. We talk.

Connie. Well, don't.   The Shays are bad news. I don't want you near them at all. I don't know why they keep coming back.

Hannah. I like Manny.

Connie. I don't care if you like the man in the moon. It's over—as of now. I don't want you associating with Shays.

Regina. This is all disturbing.

Ezekiel. The Shays are no good.

Claus. They're not anybody to be associated with.

Joey. German.

Claus. Shut up.

Oscar. Life is not as fair as it could be. I don't know if you know this, but I used to be a boxer.

Willa. I've heard that.

Oscar. I made quite a living at it. Even taught Manny how to throw a few punches. I was good in my time. Until, until I left it.

Ezekiel. His father was that killer boxer.

Julian. Killer boxer?

Sally Mae. A single blow!

Ezekiel. Yes, he killed a man with his fist! Freak!

Regina. Was that proved?

Ezekiel. Proved? It happened!

Sally Mae. Yes, it happened.

Joey. Death by fist.

Oscar. There is so much that I remember, and so much that I don't about all those years.

Ezekiel. Hit the man. Killed him. He left boxing forever. Roams the land. He was originally from here. I remember his old man. He should have left forever, but he shows up yet again.

Connie. You know, that Shay man, Oscar, asked me to marry *him* a long time ago.

Hannah. Mr. Shay?

Connie. Don't act so surprised.

Sally Mae. This town was not always a bastion of morality. There used to be a little hanky panky a few years ago.

Regina. Oh, those stories!

Julian. Please, continue.

Claus. Yes, do.

Oscar. Hardships are not always your fault. (*Pauses.*) When you find out that the one you, the one . . .you love is unfaithful.

Connie. But it's hard when you find out that someone you love—yes, I said love—has been unfaithful to you.

Ezekiel. Ah, that Holloway man with that Oscar Shay's wife! Yes. Disgusting!

Julian. That Manny boy's mother?

Connie. I don't want you blaming the Shay men folk for that part of it. I just don't think, though, that we need to be having anything to do with them. It was that woman of *his*, she cheated on him just like I was cheated on.

Oscar. That man, Holloway: he stole my wife from me.

Connie. She stole him.

Sally Mae. That Holloway man just wooed that Shay woman right off her feet.

Ezekiel. She didn't resist none, neither!

Oscar. But then to have the unthinkable happen. I'm not getting into it.

Connie. Then to have the man you love make so final a decision. No hope of any future.

Ezekiel. It's amazing how quickly passion turns to murder.

Willa. What are you talking about, Mr. Shay?

Oscar. Nothing. Nothing. (*in emotional pain*) Loss. More than one. Not just lost loyalty, loss of hope.

Connie. I have something to tell you. Then maybe you'll understand why you need to keep your distance. Your father, he, he did had an affair with the Shay woman. She had been my friend.

Ezekiel. That Shay woman and the Holloway woman had been best friends in school.

Oscar. Such loss. You have to move on.

Connie. Your father did the unthinkable. He, um, he ended it in a very final way.

Sally Mae. He killed that woman. He knew he couldn't have her anymore, so he just flat-out killed her and turned the gun on himself.

Oscar. You have to go on. For the sake of your son, you have to go on.

Connie. Your father, he took care of it and then took care of himself.

Hannah. Are you saying . . . ? Are you saying? Did he?

Connie. I'm saying he took care of it.

Hannah. He didn't just leave us?

Connie. He ended it once and for all. For her and for him.

Sally Mae. That's probably what's wrong with that boy. He was too young to remember, but I'm sure his dad talks about his dead mother all the time.

Willa. Does Manny know?

Oscar. Know about what?

Willa. The finality of the loss?

Oscar. He knows his mother's gone, that's all.

Willa. You haven't told him?

Oscar. Some things are better left unsaid.

Willa. Oh.

Oscar. But there's something more.

Willa. Okay.

Connie. I need to you stay away from him. There is a past there you didn't know about.

Oscar. Manny, uh, Manny's not gonna be with us forever. I thought you ought to know that.

Hannah. Manny Shay and I will be together forever!

There is suddenly a big crash of thunder. All the people on stage flinch and are startled.

Ezekiel. It's the voice of judgment!

Oscar. Bad part of the storm's almost here.

Connie. We knew it was coming. Now it's here.

Willa. I wonder where that lightning was.

Hannah. I didn't see the lightning.

Odom. I hope it don't break any of the glasses.

Julian. That was like an earthquake.

Oscar. You can always count on the weather.

Hannah. I'm gonna be sick!

Sally Mae. I hope this doesn't ruin the festival.

Regina. No! The show must go on!

Julian. (*drunken*) The show must go on!

Willa. What do you mean Manny won't be here forever? None of us will.

Hannah. I'll love him forever!

Oscar. I don't know if you two are . . . seeing each other.

Connie. I can take it then that you two are seeing each other?

Willa. Not really.

Hannah. Not really, but we will.

Connie. Well, it's gonna stop before it starts.

Willa. I don't even know if we are going to start. (*Laughs.*) It might stop before it starts.

Connie. I ain't gonna have it.

Willa. Mr. Shay, is there something you're not telling me?

Oscar. I'm not exactly an old man, but I'm not a young man either. Manny's human, too. We all have a beginning and an end.

Hannah. I can't believe you're telling me all this. You're absolutely forbidding me from any chance of anything! And telling me that my own father was a . . . murderer!

Connie. Shut your mouth!

Ezekiel. What are we doing about the Shay boy?

Julian. The Shay boy? Lucky in love, lucky in luck.

Sally Mae. It just scares me, scares me, scares me, but what is there to do. The boy hasn't broken any law. He's just freaky.

Regina. Don't forget. Some of us make the law.

Oscar. Life's too short to worry about a lot of things. I've lost two women. The first one, I asked to marry me. Her rejection was the best thing that ever happened to me. I loved another woman, and she was unfaithful. Life is short, very short. You gotta do what makes you happy.

Willa. Be honest, Mr. Shay. Is something wrong with Manny?

Oscar. When he was born, I named him Man. I liked that name: Man. But his mother called him Manny. I didn't like it at first, but it stuck. Manny, well, Manny

61

knows this a little, but he doesn't know all of it, but he, well, he has a very, very weak heart. He knows it's weak. He just doesn't know how weak it is. That's why I overprotect him. He, the doctors, and there have been a few, they say that he won't make it to forty. He can't. His heart can't take it. That's why he gets so winded and I step in and fix things.

Willa. Weak heart.

Oscar. Heart of gold, but weak. And don't go telling him the forty thing. I shouldn't have mentioned it, but I thought you needed to know if you are involved. It's nothing but right.

Claus. Sounds to me that the whole passel of those people are not good.

Regina. Yeah, it takes all types, but that Manny bothers me. He's scaring people.

Sally Mae. Yes! People *are* fearful.

Joey. He scares me.

The others stare at him.

Hannah and Bo run off separate ways, angry—Bo unseen by Connie or Hannah.

Oscar. I've been here long enough. (*He leaves—Willa is speechless.*)

Connie. Don't you dare go out in this storm!

Odom. Storm's rising.

Willa. (*Alone*) Storm's here. (*She puts on a coat and walks outside as if on a mission.*)

Scene 13. *There are two scenes/settings occurring simultaneously in this scene as well: Manny's bedroom and in the bad weather, out by the lake. It is nighttime.*

Manny is in his bed, tossing and turning some.

On the other side of the stage is Hannah, frustrated, crying, angry. If it all possible, in some way, the wind needs to be blowing.

Hannah. (*Crying*.) Why? Why this way? Did he have to ruin it for everyone? When things can't make much less sense, something else comes along? (*She cries.*)

For some strange reason, she starts singing a song, a strange enchanting, sad melody. She sings through tears. Then she hears something.

Hannah. Who's there? Who's there?

Bo. (*Entering*) Me.

Hannah. Oh, Bo. What are you . . . You've been crying.

Bo. (*Sarcastic*) So have you.

Hannah. Yes. (*She pauses and then understands that he, too, knows it all.*) Oh, I see.

Bo. Yeah. Mom sent me for you.

Hannah. I'm not coming.

Bo. Suit yourself. (*He starts to leave.*)

Hannah. You okay?

Bo. I'm fine. Be careful out here. The wind's getting worse. (*He leaves.*)

She sits.

Hannah. Be careful out here. (*She hears more noise.*) Bo, are you there? Or is it the wind?

Joey. (*Entering*) It's not Bo. And it's not the wind.

Hannah. (*Standing, visibly afraid*) Joey!

Joey. Bingo! Joey is my name. It is. It is! You are the bright one.

Hannah. What are you doing out here with a storm blowing up?

Joey. What are you doing out here with a storm blowing up?

Hannah. Well, . . .

Joey. Looking for men?

Hannah. What?

Joey. Looking for men, I said. That's your goal, your reason, your focus, your purpose of breathing and walking!

Hannah. No, I don't know where you got that, but it's completely wrong. I'm just . . . .

Joey. That's not what I heard. I heard you go after men left and right and then drop them.

Hannah. What?

Joey. Oh don't play dumb, Cleopatra! You know you want a good man, but you don't want him to stick around. You're not into the long-term. That's the problem with other people. They're crazy. They don't live for the here and now! I saw you out here with that Manny freak.

Hannah. Joey. I need to go home.

Joey. Oh, no. Not yet. I'm like you. I don't want love. You don't have to break my heart like you did that movie star. I don't have a weak heart. I want the here and now.

He approaches her.

Hannah. No, Joey!

He grabs her arms and the blouse rips.

Hannah. NO! (*She pulls away hard, falls, and hits her head on a rock. She is unconscious.*)

Joey looks and gets scared.

Joey. Hannah?

He runs.

There is a knock at Manny's window. Groggily, he gets up and answers it. It is Willa.

Manny. Willa? What are you . . . ?

Willa. Shh.

Manny. Willa, this is my bedroom.

Willa. I know.

She takes off her jacket and leads him to the bed.

Manny. What are you doing?

She slips off her shoes—or some other obvious article of clothing.

Willa. No more talk. Lie down.

Manny. What?

She kisses him passionately on the mouth and pushes him back on the bed.

The lights fade.

Scene 14. *On the street. Manny, tired, is carrying a blade, or a mechanical lawnmower part to the machine shop for repair. Ezekiel meets him. It is still raining.*

Ezekiel. You're walking the streets today?

Manny. It's a free country.

Ezekiel. For those who commit crimes?

Manny. What are you talking about?

Ezekiel. Did you do it?

Manny. Do what?

Ezekiel. It's one thing to be a freak, knowing things nobody has any business knowing. It's another to assault a woman!

Manny. Are you crazy? What are you talking about?

Ezekiel. That Holloway girl. Did you do it?

Manny. Holloway? Hannah?

Ezekiel. Ah, you do know her!

Manny. Tell me, old man! What happened?

Ezekiel. She's unconscious. Found her by the lake. Looks like someone tried to have their way with her or something.

Manny. Where is she?!?

Ezekiel. Hospital. Nobody can go!

Manny starts to walk away deliberately.

Ezekiel. Did you do it?

Manny. (*Turning.*) No, sir. But I have a good idea who did.   (*He exits.*)

Scene 15: *The Country Club*

Odom is working. Julian is drinking. Claus and Sally Mae enter.

Julian. Tweedle Dee . . .

Claus. What?

Sally Mae. Julian, three more of those visions have come true.

Odom. Do you go around researching all this?

Sally Mae. Yes! I work like a TV reporter.

Julian. There's something to all this. It's rubbish, a pack of lies.

Manny enters. All of them are shocked.

Sally Mae. Manny Shay!

Claus. Manny?

Julian. What are you doing here?

Claus. If you need work, the marina's next door. (*He laughs*.)

Manny. (*to Julian*) I came for you.

Julian. For me? What are you talking about?

Manny. (*Approaching*). You know exactly what I'm talking about. You wanted her. She told you no. She refused you.

Odom. Whoops.

Manny. But you couldn't accept no for an answer.

Julian. I don't know what you are talking about. I think you need to leave before we call security.

Manny. Call security. Go ahead. Find a girl in the woods. If she won't agree to being with you, you have to force her. (*He shoves Julian*.)

Julian. Don't touch me. And if you are talking about Hannah Holloway, I had nothing to do with it.

Manny. I'm sure.

Julian. I didn't do it. Yes, she turned me down, but I didn't hurt her.

Manny. Not then.

Julian. Not ever! Now leave, boy!

Manny. Fight.

Julian. (*Laughing*) Do you know who you're talking to?

Manny. A two-bit actor who moves to nowhere and rapes innocent young women?

Julian punches Manny in the stomach.

Julian. No, a trained fighter. A trained fighter.

Manny punches him.

Manny. I can hold my own. Now why'd you do it? Couldn't handle being told no?

He punches Julian again. It turns into an all-out fistfight. Halfway through, Ezekiel enters. The fight goes into slow motion. There is a pause as Manny begins to deliver a final, powerful blow.

Ezekiel. The death blow!

Julian falls to the floor, unconscious. Manny walks out slowly, exhausted.

Sally Mae. (*looking at Julian, yelling at Manny*) What have you done?

Manny exits.

Scene 16: *The Festival*

Regina is dressed up, pacing. Claus enters.

Claus. Are you okay?

Regina. Okay? Um, no. Not at all. Julian's in the hospital almost dead. The president of the Screen Actors' Guild is on his way back from the hospital. Coming here. Here.

Claus. It'll be fine. I promise.

Regina. You promise? You promise? I need a drink.

Sally Mae. (*Entering.*) Here's a Coca-Cola.

Regina. (*Takes it reluctantly and drinks.*) People actually drink this stuff?

Tom approaches.

Regina. Oh, Tom. Are you ready?

Tom. Pretty much. I don't know what to say.

Regina. That you are happy to be the recipient of the Founders' Day Citizenship Award, etcetera, etcetera, etcetera.

Tom. Why me again?

Regina. Julian's not here. I need a speech. You're a successful businessman who draws people to Lake Shiloh!

Claus. You can be it!

Sally Mae. Do it.

Claus. Ya, do it.

Tom. Is Julian going to live?

Regina. I don't know. He's in ICU now. If he dies, I'll make sure Manny Shay gets the death penalty!

Scene 17:   *On the banks of Lake Shiloh.*

Oscar, distraught, is standing. Manny, in pain, weak, furtively approaches.

Oscar. Manny!

Manny. Shh. I see you got my note.

Oscar. Yeah. What's going on? What did you do?

Manny. I fought someone too cowardly to pick on someone his own size.

Oscar. But the girl?

Manny. Julian attacked Hannah.

Oscar. People are saying it was you—and that you then went to kill Julian!

Manny. And you believe that?

Oscar. No. But I thought you and Willa?

Manny. Well, that's a long story.

Oscar. Are you okay? You look dead.

Manny. I feel dead.

Oscar. You need sleep.

Manny. Where?

Oscar. We have to do something. You didn't attack that girl?

Manny. Dad, no! Never. I actually had some special feelings for her.

Oscar. Well, she may never recover. It was a bad blow she took to the head. Almost as bad the blow you gave that movie star!

Manny. Dad, I had to!

Oscar. I didn't teach you to . . ..

Manny. Dad!

Oscar. What?

Manny. Believe me. If no one else does, believe me.

Oscar. (*Pauses.*) Okay. To the ends of the earth.

Manny hugs him.

Oscar. You're in trouble, though. You're considered a fugitive, and if you get caught, you're going to jail.

Manny. I know. I'm just so tired. (*Sinks to the ground, puts his head in his hands.)*

Oscar. Well, you've got two choices. You can turn yourself in, tell 'em what happened, or you can run.

Manny. Tell 'em what happened?

Oscar. Yeah! That you had nothing to do with what happened to that Holloway girl, that that was the reason you went to see Julian Fletcher, to see if he had done it.

Manny. Who else could have done it?! Dad, she rejected him! He wanted her. She turned him down because she wanted to . . . be with me.

Oscar. Well, I believe you, but whatever, whatever the case, there are four witnesses that say they saw you pick a fight and use, well, excessive force.

Manny. How is she?

Oscar. The last I heard, she's still in the hospital, still unconscious, her and that movie star both. (Pauses.) What about Willa?

Manny. (*Frustrated*.) Oh, Dad, I don't know. It's amazing how life can be moving along so comfortably, then two or three or four or five things just come out of nowhere and just (*He is out of breath*) . . . just knock you over.

Oscar. I know, son.

Manny. I guess I need to talk to her.

Oscar. How you gonna do that?

Manny. I need to find her.

Oscar. Well, son, she's probably at the festival, and I don't know if I'd go there if I were you!

Manny. Don't you have faith in me?

Oscar. Yeah, I do. More than you realize.

Manny. I never claimed to be able to walk on water. I never claimed to be able to do much, but all I know to do is to do what's right. I gotta find her.

Oscar. Well, let's find you something different to wear. I wish this storm would stop, or at least make up its mind. It just keeps coming and going.

Manny. Yeah, I've never seen the lake quite this high.

Oscar. Let's find you something to wear.

They exit.

Scene 18: *The Founders' Day Festival.*

Claus and Sally Mae are standing stage left looking off into the wings. They are listening to the speech Tom Ortiz is giving.

Tom. (*offstage—stage left*) And in conclusion, I want to thank the people of Lake Shiloh for choosing me, for their confidence in me as their recipient of the citizenship award. I take great pride in running my marina in a manner that makes you all proud to be residents of Lake Shiloh. Again, thank you! Thank you very much.

We hear applause. Claus and Sally Mae clap, too.

Regina. (*Offstage—stage left*) Thank you, Tom Ortiz, for your beautiful speech.

Tom enters from stage left.

Tom. (*to Claus and Sally Mae*) I'm glad that's over. Speechmaking makes me nervous.

Claus. You did fine.

Sally Mae. You were great.

Regina. (*offstage*) We are very proud to have Tom in our community. He is an upstanding citizen and someone who helps define the very character and nature of Lake Shiloh.

Applause—even Claus and Sally Mae.

Regina. The last few days have been difficult ones for the denizens of Lake Shiloh. The weather hasn't exactly cooperated with our best-laid plans. As best as we can tell, the storms are beginning to subside. Other situations will improve as time progresses as well. I do appreciate you "weathering the weather." (*She laughs.*) And we hope the rest of your time as the festival is wonderful. Get out and spend some money and have some fun. Enjoy! The dance will commence at 9 o'clock. Good afternoon and good bye!

Applause.

Regina enters to the area where Claus, Sally Mae, and Tom are standing.

Regina. I've never been so tongue-tied in my entire life.

Sally Mae. You sounded fine. You sounded calm and cool and sophisticated.

Willa wanders onto the upstage center area. She is unaware of the others. They are unaware of her. She stares, thinks, shows nervousness.

Joey saunters in to join Regina, Claus, and the rest. They are uncomfortable with his presence.

Joey. You really, you really ought to consider a run, a run for the President!

Regina. Why thank you, Joey. I'll keep that in mind.

Joey. I tell you. This rain's starting to get to me, to get to me, though. It's just, it's just, just made the lake rise. It's done quite a few things.

Regina. Well, it's pretty obvious that it's brought with it quite a few things that are unwelcome in our community.

Joey. Froggie went a-courting, and he did ride, uh-huh.

Claus. Would you please stop that!

Joey. (*Saluting.*) Ya Vole!

Regina. This town was perfectly fine until the outcast came into out midst.

Oscar and Manny enter stage right and stand, nervously, upstage right. They are dressed in odd clothes, coats, hats, etc. They are looking at Willa.

Oscar notices Willa. He motions for Manny to stay put while he goes to get Willa. He walks to her. She is startled, but she realizes who it is. He points over to Manny. She looks hopeful and runs over to him. The others are still unaware.

Willa. Manny! Where have you been? Are you all right? You look like death warmed over.

Manny. I don't have a lot of time to talk. I need to hit the road. But, um, . . . (*He is tired.*)

Willa. Hit the road? You're leaving?

Manny. Yeah. They . . . Dad told me that they think I'm the one who hurt Hannah.

Willa. You couldn't have done that!

Manny. I didn't. Fletcher had to have done it. Hannah told me that he wanted her to, that he wanted her attention, but that she, well, she refused. It was him. A man who has everything turned down.

Willa. You did go after Julian?

Manny. Yeah. I did. He denied it.

Ezekiel enters stage right, joining Regina and the others.

Ezekiel. He's dead!

Regina. What?

Claus. Who?

Sally Mae. No!

Ezekiel. Julian! Julian Fletcher just died.

Regina. (*Grabbing a handkerchief*) Murderer.

Claus. Why hasn't the law picked that boy up yet?

Sally Mae. They've been looking everywhere.

Joey. Ain't looked hard enough.

Ezekiel. I tell you! He's a freak. He was a freak the first day I laid eyes on him. He's like his old man. Scaring people half to death is one thing, but to kill 'em , to *kill* people! (*He now screams*) Manny Shay is a murderer, and he'll pay! Manny Shay is a murderer, and he'll pay!

Manny, Oscar, and Willa look up and over in the direction of Ezekiel. They heard his cry.

Willa. Oh, no.

Oscar. Julian must have died.

Manny. I guess I know what that means.

Oscar. There's no hope now.

Regina. The most famous man in town, and he's dead, killed by a freak, a total pariah. Anybody got a drink?

Joey hands her a flask. She looks at it skeptically, sniffs it, and then drinks it.

Sally Mae. This is horrible, horrible. A horrible day in Lake Shiloh!

There is an scream by an off-stage actor.

Regina. What's wrong?

Claus. (*Pointing offstage, upstage left*) Look!

Sally Mae. It's someone drowning!

Regina. Drowning?

Ezekiel. It's a sign!

Claus. That poor man is drowning.

Willa, Oscar, and Manny, hearing this, reluctantly move closer.

Regina. Well, is anyone going to help him!

Joey. I can't.

Claus. I can't swim.

Sally Mae. Oh, my!

Ezekiel. It's a sign!

Regina. Is no one going into to help that poor man!

Manny. Dad!

Oscar. Manny.

Manny. Dad, no one?

Oscar. Manny. (Scared)

Willa. Manny?

Sally Mae. He's not going to make it!

Manny. Dad!

Oscar. (*Gives in.*) GO!

Weak and stripping some of his clothes, Manny runs toward the lake—offstage left.

Claus. Is that . . . ?

Regina. That's the freak?

Sally Mae. Manny Shay?

Ezekiel. Manny Shay? Manny Shay?

Oscar. Man Shay.

Manny pulls Bo up onstage. They are both wet and can barely breathe.

Ezekiel. Manny Shay?

Claus. That's, that's the Holloway girl's brother!

Sally Mae. Bo?

Oscar and Willa tend to Manny, try to get him on his feet.

The rest tend to Bo.

Claus. (*to Bo*) What happened?

Regina. What were you doing out there in the lake?

Bo. (*Breathless*) My boat capsized.

Regina. Boat? On that water? I need another drink. (*Looking around.*)

Sally Mae. Are you all right?

Bo. I don't know.

Sally Mae. You look horrible.

Bo. (*Standing*) I've been, been thinking. Thinking about a lot of things.

Willa and Oscar have Manny on his feet, but he is weak.

Connie runs up.

Connie. (*Hugging Bo.*) Bo! You're alive! I thought you weren't going to make it.

Bo. What are you doing here? Aren't you supposed to be at the hospital?

Connie. I was there. I was coming home to get you. She's gonna be okay, Bo. She's gonna be okay. She's coming out of it. And then, I come here, and you're almost drowned.

Joey gets a look of horror on his face when she says that Hannah will be all right. He runs off, stage right. They look.

Bo. (*To his mother*) Let go of me. (*He pulls away. He is changed, disgusted, angry.*)

Connie. You almost drowned!

Ezekiel. He would have drowned if it hadn't been for Manny Shay.

Manny, supported by Oscar turns to face Bo.

Bo. (*With shock and anger on his face.*) What?

Sally Mae. Manny's the one who went in and saved you.

Bo is extremely angry.

Manny. Don't worry about it, Bo. Nobody was going in. I couldn't let you drown.

Bo, getting angrier, turns away from Manny. Connie grabs Bo's arm. He yanks her hand off of him. Oscar turns Manny to the side, facing stage right.

Oscar. Let's get you dried off and find you a place to rest a few minutes.

Bo pulls some sort of large knife out of his pocket and briskly walks toward the very weak Manny.

Bo. Hey, freak!

Before Manny can stop him, he shoves the knife into Manny's upper abdomen. (This action should be done in slow motion.)

Oscar, Willa, and Connie all scream "NO!"

Manny falls to the ground. Oscar and Willa try to hold him up. They both start crying.

Connie. Bo! No! Why?

The others are in shock, almost frozen. Bo looks at the knife, then at Manny.

Manny. (*Looking at Bo.*) Bo? Bo? (*His breathing is getting harder.*)

Bo then stabs the knife in his own abdomen, in the same place he stabbed Manny.

Connie screams.

Bo falls. Connie holds him.

Manny. Bo?

Bo. (*Looking at Manny*) You're not the only freak.

Connie. No, no. This can't be happening.

Oscar. (*Crying*) Manny? Manny? Listen to me. Can you hear me? It can't end this way. This wasn't supposed to happen. Manny?

Manny. Dad?

Oscar. Yes, Manny, yes!

Manny. Dad. So much for a weak heart. (*He dies.*)

Oscar. Manny!

Bo dies as well.

Connie screams.

Everyone else stares.

Scene 19. *Willa's gift shop. Six weeks have passed. Willa is dusting. Oscar enters with a suitcase and is dressed in traveling clothes.*

Willa. Oscar!

Oscar. Willa, sweetheart.

Willa. Are you still insisting on leaving?

Oscar. We've discussed this. I've been here several weeks too long. I can't stay here. I have to, well, I just have to go. Now that they've found Joey Argo, I can rest.

Willa. Okay.

Oscar. A little over six weeks ago, I lost the most important thing in my life. I just can't . . . (*He chokes up.)*

Willa. (*Comforting him.*) I know, Oscar. And if you need to go on to Timbuktu, you do that! You just promise to come back here and see me.

Oscar. (*Painfully, yet sincerely)* I will. *(Pauses.)* Well, keep the business open! And try to stay clear of those weirdoes all over the town.

Willa. (*Laughing*) I will. You know you're welcome to come and stay with me any time you want. You can now even!

Oscar. I know. I know. But I gotta do what I gotta do.

Willa. Okay.

He starts walking toward the door. She walks with him. They arrive on the sidewalk.

Oscar. Well, this is it. Good-bye, sweetheart. I'll see you in . . . a few months.

He hugs her.

Willa. You call me!

Oscar. Okay. (*He leaves.)*

She stands in the sidewalk, looking around, puts both hands on her belly and looks down.

Hannah wearing a headscarf and using a cane approaches.

Willa. (*Uncomfortably, yet gently)* Hannah.

Hannah. (*Strained as well*) How are you?

Willa. Surviving. How's rehab going?

Hannah. I should be without this thing (*holds up the cane*) in another three weeks. Other than that, I am doing much better. I just moved into a room at the

Hollister and, I'll be on the sidewalks bothering people with my reading in no time.

They both laugh. Again, there is obvious tension and discomfort.

Hannah. (*Slowly*) Did I just see Oscar leave?

Willa. Yeah. He'll be back, though.

Hannah. I know.

Willa. Listen, would you care for some lunch at the Marina? My treat. If you can't, don't worry. No pressure.

Hannah. (*Although it is obviously strained and difficult, she tries to be cordial.*) That would be "right-near" kind of you.

Willa. Let me lock up. (*She takes keys from her pocket and locks the door.*) There. Sealed up. Locked.

Hannah. Safe and sound.

Willa. Safe and sound. Let's go.

They walk toward stage left. Willa stops. Hannah follows suit. Willa looks back at the stage then to Hannah.

Willa. Safe and sound.

She puts her arms around Hannah's shoulder, and they walk off stage left.

Music crescendos as they exit.

Lights fade.

Lowery Christopher Collins (Chris) has been an educator and writer for over thirty years. He is currently a professor of English at Panola College in Carthage, Texas. He has taught at the high school, middle school, and elementary school levels and as an English and literature instructor at the college and university level. For several years, he was a high school theatre director and a gifted education consultant. He's been honored with several teaching awards, including the Young Audiences of Northeast Texas Outstanding Service to the Profession Award and the Kennedy Center's Steven Sondheim Award for being one of the most "Inspirational Teachers" in the U.S.

He is also an award-winning playwright of over thirty scripts, a weekly newspaper columnist, a short story writer, a poet, a pianist, a vocalist, a songwriter, a recording artist with Daywind Studios, the founder and artistic director of Stagelands Theatre Company, an aspiring novelist, and a (former) choir director. He's taught a variety of classes, from rhetoric and composition to literature to acting to the Bible.

He holds a Bachelor of Arts Degree in English and History and a Master of Arts Degree in English from Stephen F. Austin State University in Texas and has served on fine arts and gifted education committees as well as on a board of governors for a small playhouse.

In addition to his interests in teaching, directing, and writing, he has a fondness for lighthouses, windmills, filmmaking, salsa, sculpture, Flannery O'Connor, travel, dominos, guacamole, social media, genetics, Maine, landscaping, pillows, gospel music, Shakespeare, marbles, YouTube, quantum physics, movies, weird jokes, maps, trees, cold rooms, and Texas.

He can be reached at mrchriscollins@hotmail.com,

on Facebook at www.facebook.com/tofferdreams,

on Twitter at "tofferdreams,"

and at his website: www.ChristopherCollinsOnline.com.

To view Christopher Collins's books and other writing, visit Ponderlake Publishing, at www.ponderlake.com.